Chabad's Desert Torah Academy
1312 Vista Drive
Las Vegas, NV 89102
702-259-1000

SAT ON A HAT

By Bracha Goetz
Illustrated by Dena Ackerman

This book is dedicated to my precious grandchildren.
May each of you be blessed to find joy throughout life! - BG

With tremendous appreciation to my art mentor, Marc Lumer. - DA

Copyright © 2014 by Israel Bookshop Publications

ISBN 978-1-60091-342-6

Art direction and book design: Marc Lumer

Published by:
Israel Bookshop Publications
501 Prospect Street
Lakewood, NJ 08701
Tel: (732) 901-3009
Fax: (732) 901-4012

www.israelbookshoppublications.com
info@israelbookshoppublications.com

Printed in China

Distributed in Israel by:
Shanky's
Petach Tikva 16
Jerusalem
972-2-538-6936

Distributed in Australia by:
Gold's Book and Gift Company
3- 13 William Street
Balaclava 3183
613-9527-8775

Distributed in Europe by:
Lehmanns
Unit E Viking Industrial Park
Rolling Mill Road,
Jarrow , Tyne & Wear NE32 3DP
44-191-430-0333

Distributed in South Africa by:
Kollel Bookshop
Northfield Centre
17 Northfield Avenue
Glenhazel 2192
27-11-440-6679

Got my first hat!
How about that?

P ut it on a chair.
Did it jump in the air?

Did I leave it at school?

Or the coat rack at shul?

I is it on this high shelf?

I can't reach there myself!

W hat's behind my clock?
Found a missing sock!

I really don't think
I put it in the sink.

And not in a pot.
Then my hat would be HOT!

And I have a strong feeling,
It's not on the ceiling.

Is it under the rug?
Hope I don't find a bug!

No, it's not on the floor.

Did it get out the door?

Did it land in the van?
I can look there. I can.

If it went in a car,
It could go very far.

It could land on a duck
In a blue pick-up truck.

And that duck, on a bus,

Would make such a fuss!

Maybe it got stuck
On a red fire truck.

But a fireman's hat
Would not look like that!

What if it's on a boat?
Hats can't swim. Can they float?

Maybe it's on a train.

It could be on a plane.

Hope it's not on the moon.
I hope I find it soon!

It could land on a tree,
And then land back on me.

I've looked all over town.
Now I must sit down.

Oh! What have I found?
Something black and round!

Just as I wished!
My hat! (A bit squished!)